For Hannah, Jim and the real Stella

First published in 2014 by Child's Play (International) Ltd
Ashworth Road, Bridgemead, Swindon SN5 7YD UK

Published in USA by Child's Play Inc
250 Minot Avenue, Auburn, Maine 04210

Distributed in Australia by Child's Play Australia Pty Ltd
Unit 10/20 Narabang Way, Belrose, NSW 2085

Text and illustrations copyright © 2014 Courtney Dicmas
The moral right of the author/illustrator has been asserted

ISBN 978-1-84643-639-0
CLP170913CPL10136390

Printed in Shenzhen, China

1 3 5 7 9 10 8 6 4 2

A catalogue record of this book
is available from the British Library

www.childs-play.com

The Great Googly Moogly

Courtney Dicmas

Stella was a small girl who dreamt of catching a BIG fish.

But not just any fish would do.
The Great Googly Moogly was the biggest fish of them all.

It had terrible jaws...

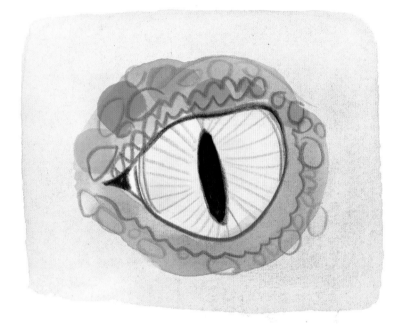

...and horrible yellow eyes
the size of dinner plates.

For two hundred years, no one had been able to reel it in.

This didn't stop Stella. Every day, she went down to the dock to catch the Googly Moogly...

...and every day was the same.

The wind rolled.

The waves lapped.

But no fish would bite.

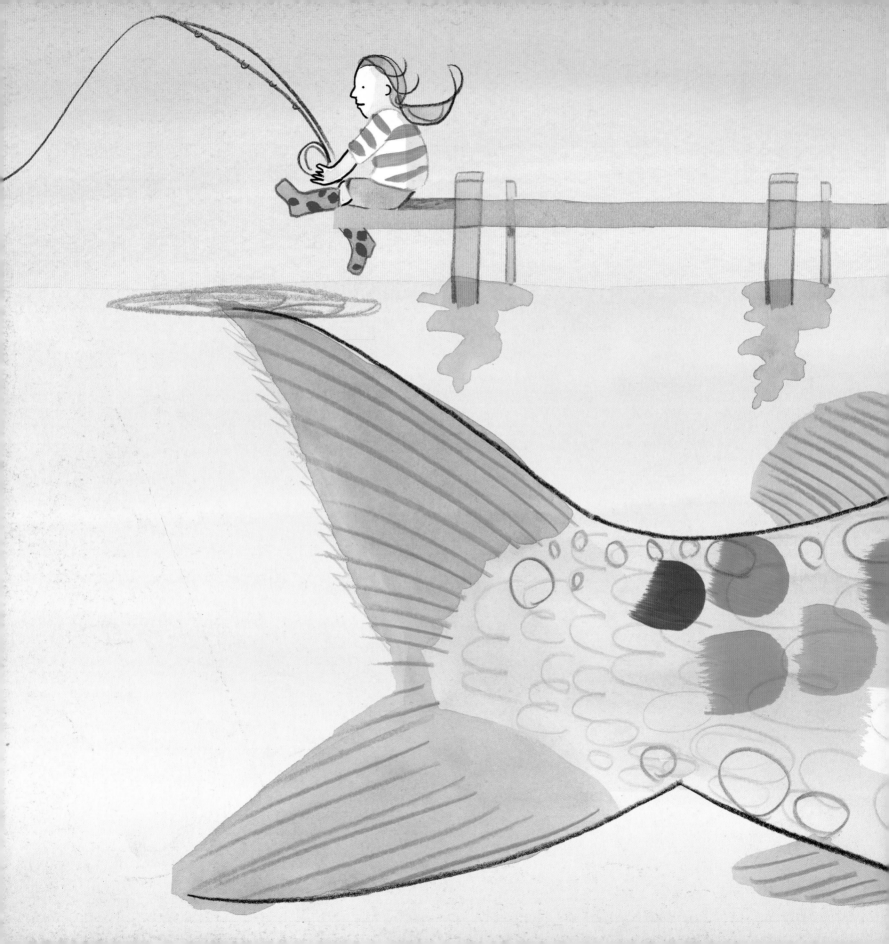

Not even a nibble.

At dinner each day, it seemed Stella caught everything except what she was looking for.

In her dreams, she wished for the Googly Moogly.
It was hers to catch.

Stella just wouldn't give up.

She tried fly fishing.

She bought new bait.

She was patient through the rain.

But still there was no Googly Moogly in sight.

So, like any expert, she had lunch and took a short nap.

Stella awoke to
the soft *ker-ploosh*
of water on her head.

"WAIT! Where are your yellow eyes?"

SLURP!

"Where are your terrible jaws?"

Suddenly, the Great Googly Moogly
took a Great Moogly leap.

Down
they
plunged...

...scattering

seaweed...

...and

stirring up

starfish...

...up into the light,
where things looked different
to Stella somehow.

She had done it - caught it at LAST! Well sort of.
But was the Googly Moogly hers to keep?

Stella wasn't sure.

In her heart, she knew
what she had to do.

That night, Stella was quiet.
She missed the Googly Moogly.

She dreamt of the Great Googly Moogly
swimming in the wide open sea.

Tomorrow she would go down
to the water and enjoy the sunshine.
Perhaps the Googly Moogly would be there?

And it was!
From that day on, Stella was
happy not to catch another fish.

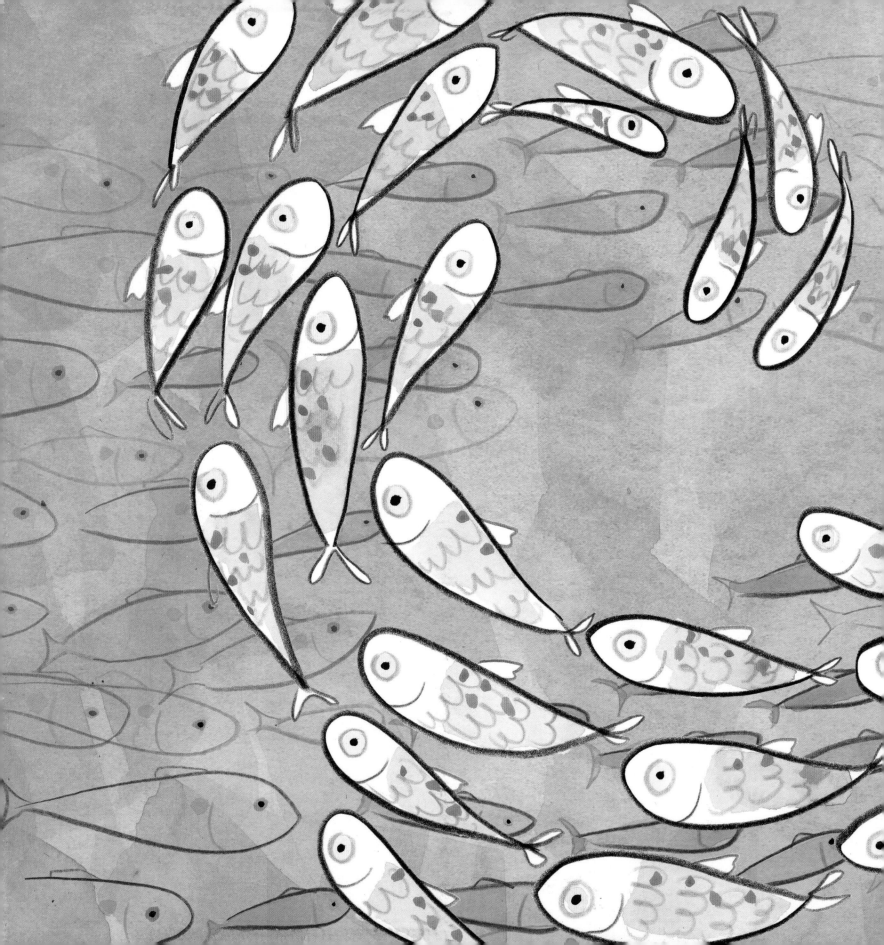